Dear Parent:

Your child's love of reading starts here!

Every child learns to read in a different way and at his or her own speed. Some go back and forth between reading levels and read favorite books again and again. Others read through each level in order. You can help your young reader improve and become more confident by encouraging his or her own interests and abilities. From books your child reads with you to the first books he or she reads alone, there are I Can Read Books for every stage of reading:

SHARED READING
Basic language, word repetition, and whimsical illustrations, ideal for sharing with your emergent reader

BEGINNING READING
Short sentences, familiar words, and simple concepts for children eager to read on their own

READING WITH HELP
Engaging stories, longer sentences, and language play for developing readers

READING ALONE
Complex plots, challenging vocabulary, and high-interest topics for the independent reader

I Can Read Books have introduced children to the joy of reading since 1957. Featuring award-winning authors and illustrators and a fabulous cast of beloved characters, I Can Read Books set the standard for beginning readers.

A lifetime of discovery begins with the magical words "I Can Read!"

Visit www.icanread.com for information
on enriching your child's reading experience.

The Berenstain Bears' Big Track Meet
Copyright © 2020 by Berenstain Publishing, Inc.
All rights reserved. Manufactured in China.
No part of this book may be used or reproduced in any manner whatsoever without written permission except
in the case of brief quotations embodied in critical articles and reviews. For information address HarperCollins
Children's Books, a division of HarperCollins Publishers, 195 Broadway, New York, NY 10007.
www.icanread.com

Library of Congress Control Number: 2019936836
ISBN 978-0-06-265472-4 (trade bdg.) — ISBN 978-0-06-265471-7 (pbk.)

Book design by Chrisila Maida
20 21 22 23 24 SCP 10 9 8 7 6 5 4 3 2 1
❖
First Edition

I Can Read!

1 BEGINNING READING

The Berenstain Bears'®
BIG TRACK MEET

Mike Berenstain

Based on the characters created by
Stan and Jan Berenstain

HARPER
An Imprint of HarperCollinsPublishers

The Bear family's big track meet
starts today!

Papa, Sister, and Brother are in the games.

Mama is the coach.

Honey cheers them on.

It's time to run a race.

"Ready, get set, run!" says Mama.

Papa runs fast.

Brother runs faster.

But Sister runs fastest!

She is the best runner.

Sister wins the race.

Sister gets the gold medal.

Brother gets the silver medal.

Papa gets the bronze medal.

Now it's time for the long jump.

"Ready, get set, jump!" says Mama.

Papa jumps far.

Sister jumps farther.

But Brother jumps farthest!

He is the best jumper.

Brother wins the long jump.

This time,

Brother gets the gold medal.

Sister gets the silver medal.

But Papa still gets the bronze medal.

The Bear family is ready for the rope climb.

"Ready, get set, climb!" says Mama.

Papa climbs high.

Brother climbs higher.

But Sister climbs highest!

She is the best climber.

Sister wins the rope climb.

Poor Papa!

Won't he EVER do something the best?

It's time for the diving contest.

"Ready, get set, dive!" says Mama.

Papa dives with a splash.

Sister dives with a smaller splash.

18

But Brother dives with the

smallest splash!

He is the best diver.

Brother wins the diving contest.

"Let's swing on the rings," says Mama.

"Ready, get set, swing!"

Papa swings some.

Brother swings more.

But Sister swings the most!

She is the best swinger.

Sister wins the ring swing.

It's time for the high jump.

"Ready, get set, leap!" says Mama.

Papa goes under the bar.

Sister goes into the bar.

But Brother goes over the bar!

He is the best leaper.

Brother wins the high jump.

"I'm tired!" says Sister.

"I'm very tired!" says Brother.

"I'm very, very tired!" says Papa.

Poor Papa!

Won't he EVER do something the best?

It's time for a nap.

"Ready, get set, sleep!" whispers Mama.

They all go to sleep.

Sister sleeps long.

She is a good sleeper.

Brother sleeps longer.

He is a better sleeper.

Papa's still asleep!

He is the best sleeper.

Papa wins the nap!

"Hooray! Hooray!" everyone shouts.

"There is something Papa Bear does the best!

He is the best napper of them all!"

"ZZZZZ!" says Papa Bear.